Gonzo the Great

D0450855

by Marilyn Kaye
illustrated by Lauren Attinello

SCHOLASTIC INC.
New York Toronto London Auckland Sydney

For Mariek,
with love from her godmother—
Marilyn Kaye

ISBN 0-590-40706-6

12 11 10 9 8 7 6 5 4 3 2 1   9/8 0 1 2 3 4/9

Printed in the U.S.A.   23

First Scholastic printing, February 1989

Gonzo was having a wonderful dream.
Crowds of people were clapping and
cheering for him.
"Hooray for Gonzo the Great!
Hooray for Gonzo the Great!"
they shouted.

Then Gonzo woke up.
But he was still thinking about his dream.
"I don't want to be just plain Gonzo anymore,"
he told Camilla.
"I need a great new act so I can be
Gonzo the Great."

Gonzo made breakfast.
He was very hungry, so he ate
lots and lots of oatmeal.
And suddenly, he had an idea
for an act.

He jumped up and ran to
Kermit's house.
On the way, he saw Fozzie
hurrying up the street.
"Hey, Fozzie! Guess what?

I am going to juggle twelve bowls
of oatmeal without spilling a drop.
Don't you think that will be a great act?"

"It's okay," said Fozzie.
"I have to go to the store.
See you later."
Gonzo sighed.
He didn't want to be Gonzo the Okay.
He wanted to be Gonzo the Great.
He needed a better act.

When he got to Kermit's house,
Robin was coming out the door.

"Hello, Robin!" Gonzo called.
"I have a new act.
    I will ride a bicycle
    and juggle twelve bowls of oatmeal
    at the same time.
    Won't that make a great act?"

"Yes, that's a nice act," Robin said.
"I have to go to school now.
'Bye, Gonzo."
Gonzo frowned.
He didn't want to be Gonzo the Nice.
He had to make the act even better.

Gonzo went into Kermit's house.
"Kermit! Where are you?"
Kermit came into the room.
"Hi, Gonzo," he said.
"I'm cleaning my basement."

"Call me Gonzo the Great!" Gonzo said.
"I have a new act.
  I am going to ride a bicycle
  on a tightrope
  and juggle twelve bowls of oatmeal
  all at the same time.
  What do you think of that?"
"That's good," Kermit said.
"I have to get back to work now.
  See you later."

Gonzo began to worry.
He didn't want to be Gonzo the Good.
He wanted to be Gonzo the Great!
What else could he do?

Just then someone rang
Kermit's doorbell.
Gonzo opened the door.
"Hi, Piggy.
Let me tell you about my new act.
I am going to ride a bicycle
on a tightrope
and juggle twelve bowls of oatmeal
while Camilla stands on my head
all at the same time."

"Not bad," said Piggy.
"Could you give these tickets to Kermit?
   They are for the circus tonight.
   Thank you, Gonzo."
And she hurried away.

Now Gonzo felt terrible.
He didn't want to be Gonzo the Not Bad.
Slowly he walked down the street.
Nobody liked his act.
No one thought he could be Gonzo
the Great.

Then he heard some music.
He followed the sounds.
He saw big tents,
with blue and yellow stripes.
It was the circus!
And suddenly, Gonzo knew how
he could become
Gonzo the Great.

That night, Kermit and Piggy and Fozzie
and Robin went to the circus.
They saw funny clowns
and dancing elephants
and acrobats flying through the air.
And then they had a big surprise.

"Ladies and gentlemen and pigs
and frogs and bears!
Presenting, for the first time
anywhere, Gonzo the Great!"

Sure enough, there was Gonzo
on the tightrope.
He was riding a bicycle
with Camilla on his head.
He was juggling twelve bowls of oatmeal.
He didn't spill a single drop!

The crowd went crazy.
They yelled and clapped and cheered.
"Hooray for Gonzo the Great!
Hooray for Gonzo the Great!"
Kermit and Piggy and Fozzie and Robin
yelled and clapped and cheered too.
They were very proud of Gonzo.

After the show, the Muppets looked for Gonzo.
"Gonzo, that was terrific!" Kermit said.
"You were wonderful!" added Fozzie.
"Let's go home and have a party for Gonzo,"
said Piggy.
"A party for me? Oh boy!" Gonzo felt
very happy.

But the ringmaster shook his head.
"You can't go now, Gonzo.
   Don't you want to travel with us?
   The circus is leaving town tonight!"
"Oh no," Fozzie exclaimed,
"you can't leave us, Gonzo."
"Please don't go away," Robin cried.
"You belong here, with your friends,"
   Kermit said.

Gonzo did not know what to do.
"What do you think?" he asked Camilla.
"Should we go with the circus
    or go home with our friends?"
"Cluck," said Camilla.
She was not much help.

"Stay with the circus!" said the ringmaster.
"Just think of it!
  The crowds will yell and clap and
  cheer for you!
  You can be Gonzo the Great every night!"

"But if you stay with us," said Kermit,
"you can be Gonzo the Great all the time."
Gonzo was surprised. "Really?"
"Yes," Kermit said.
"We *always* think you are Gonzo the Great.
Even if we don't say it."

Now Gonzo knew what to do.
"I am sorry," he told the ringmaster.
"But I want to stay with my friends."

The Muppets went home and
had a big party. They ate cookies,
and they sang songs,
and they danced.
Gonzo was very happy to be there.
Sometimes he thought about the circus.
He liked hearing the crowd call him
Gonzo the Great.

But his friends made him *feel*
like Gonzo the Great.
And that was even better.